PREVIOUSLY IN

IRON MAN®

THOR®

In the wake of the Siege of Asgard, the city lies in ruins. While Tony Stark, forgiven of all past crimes, arrives to aid the Asgardians in the reconstruction of the Shining City, dark forces are at work: the High Evolutionary has grand plans to build a god fit for the twenty-first century, by blending technology and the qualities of the divine. He's a big fan of Tony's Iron Man suit...and he plans to use Tony as the vessel for his new deity.

After a furious battle against Thor in Asgard, the troll Ulik and the evil alchemist Diablo manage to steal the Asgardian Destroyer armor and deliver it to the High Evolutionary in the conceptual space that serves as the creative headquarters for his new god—hidden in the pages of an ancient text. Thor, discovering their whereabouts, breaks in, but Diablo subdues him and Iron Man with a mind-altering potion that pits them against each other, and when they come to, they're bound to the High Evolutionary's god-machine, preparing to be sapped of all their strength.

Realizing that he can rely on no one, the High Evolutionary uses himself as the vessel for his own new god. But Diablo was never to be trusted: unknown to anyone, Diablo used his nefarious alchemical tricks to trade places and appearances with the High Evolutionary, usurping him, and transforming himself into the new deity!

DAN ABNETT & ANDY LANING
WRITERS

SCOT EATON
PENCILER

JAIME MENDOZA
INKER

VERONICA GANDINI
COLORIST

VC'S CLAYTON COWLES
LETTERS & PRODUCTION

STEPHEN SEGOVIA & JASON KEITH
COVER

CHARLIE BECKERMAN
ASST. EDITOR

RALPH MACCHIO
EDITOR

AXEL ALONSO
EDITOR IN CHIEF

JOE QUESADA
CHIEF CREATIVE OFFICER

DAN BUCKLEY
PUBLISHER

ALAN FINE
EXECUTIVE PRODUCER

visit us at www.abdopublishing.com

Reinforced library bound edition published in 2012 by Spotlight, a division of the ABDO Group, 8000 West 78th Street, Edina, Minnesota 55439. Spotlight produces high-quality reinforced library bound editions for schools and libraries. Published by agreement with Marvel Entertainment, LLC. The stories, characters, and incidents mentioned are entirely fictional.
All rights reserved. Used under authorization.

Printed in the United States of America, Melrose Park, Illinois.
052011
092011
 This book contains at least 10% recycled materials.

Library of Congress Cataloging-in-Publication Data

Abnett, Dan.
  God complex / writer: Dan Abnett & Andy Lanning ; penciler: Scot Eaton. -- Reinforced library bound ed.
     p. cm. -- (Iron Man and Thor)
  Summary: Thor, God of Thunder and heir to the ancient and mythic heritage of divine power, and Iron Man, an invincible hero and miracle of science and engineering, come together to fight a menace that is both magical and technological.
  ISBN 978-1-59961-942-2 (chapter 1) -- ISBN 978-1-59961-943-9 (chapter 2) -- ISBN 978-1-59961-944-6 (chapter 3) -- ISBN 978-1-59961-945-3 (chapter 4)
  1. Graphic novels. [1. Graphic novels. 2. Science fiction. 3. Superheroes--Fiction.] I. Lanning, Andy. II. Eaton, Scot. III. Title.
  PZ7.7.A26God 2011
  741.5'973--dc23
                       2011013485

All Spotlight books are reinforced library bindings
and manufactured in the United States of America.

VALENCIA, 1094 A.D.

THE STUDY OF ALCHEMY IS THE PURSUIT OF **TRANSFORMATION**, FOR IN CHANGE, **ALL** THINGS ARE MADE POSSIBLE.

EVEN I WAS NOT THE DIABLO YOU HAVE COME TO KNOW.

MY **OWN** HUMBLE TRANSMUTATION BEGAN DURING **EL CID'S** SIEGE OF VALENCIA.

AFTER BITTER MONTHS, THE CITY **REFUSED** TO FALL. IN AN EFFORT TO END THE STRUGGLE, EL CID TURNED TO ME...

...EVEN THOUGH HE WAS A PRAGMATIC MAN OF WAR, WITH LITTLE LIKING OF THE ESOTERIC ARTS.

THE VERY SOLDIERS SELECTED TO ESCORT ME TREATED ME WITH DISDAIN.

THEY WERE MORE AFRAID OF **ME** THAN THEY WERE OF DISCOVERY BY THE CITY DEFENDERS.

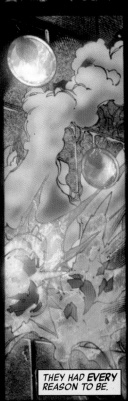

THEY HAD **EVERY** REASON TO BE.

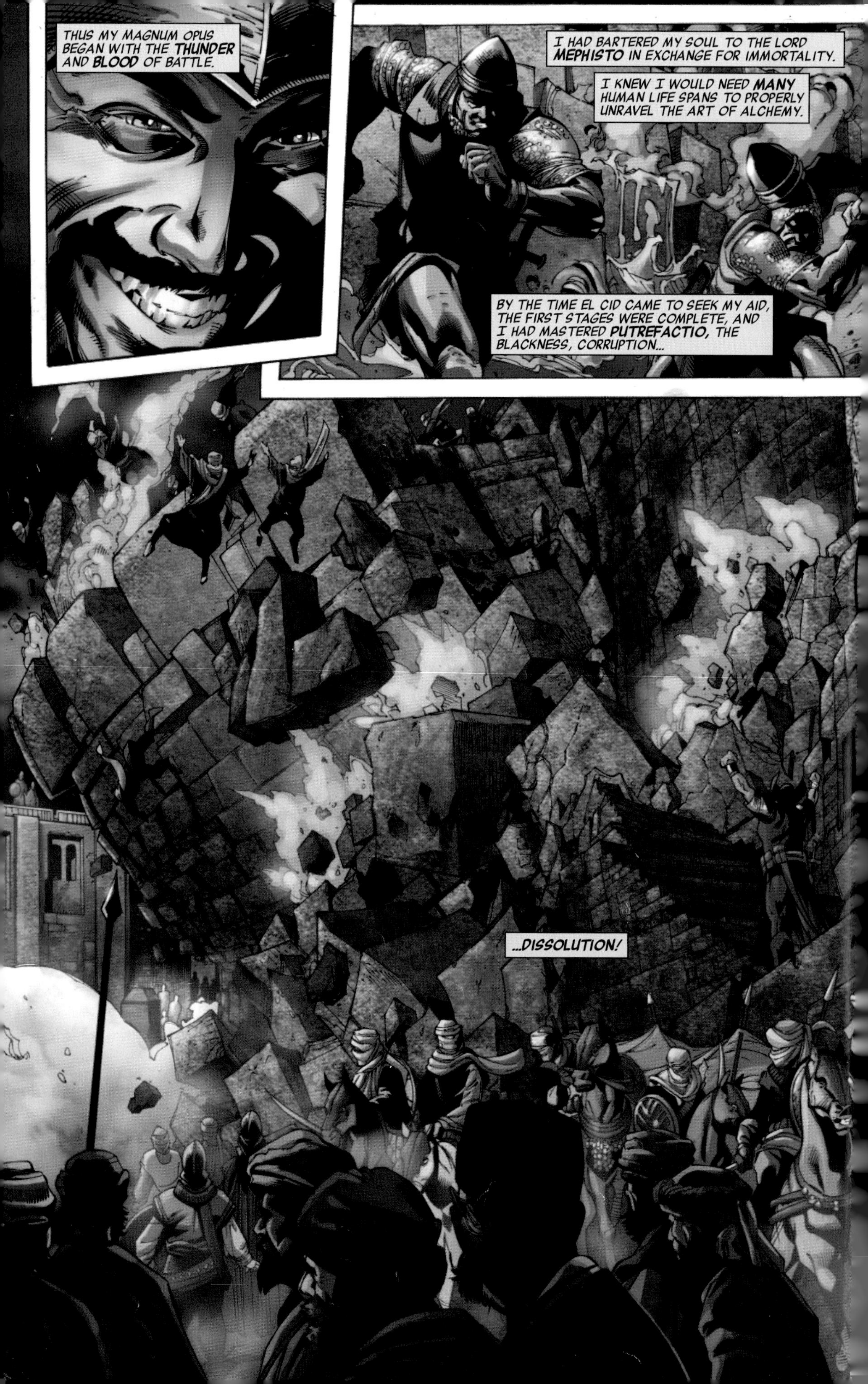
THUS MY MAGNUM OPUS BEGAN WITH THE THUNDER AND BLOOD OF BATTLE.
I HAD BARTERED MY SOUL TO THE LORD MEPHISTO IN EXCHANGE FOR IMMORTALITY.
I KNEW I WOULD NEED MANY HUMAN LIFE SPANS TO PROPERLY UNRAVEL THE ART OF ALCHEMY.
BY THE TIME EL CID CAME TO SEEK MY AID, THE FIRST STAGES WERE COMPLETE, AND I HAD MASTERED PUTREFACTIO, THE BLACKNESS, CORRUPTION...
...DISSOLUTION!

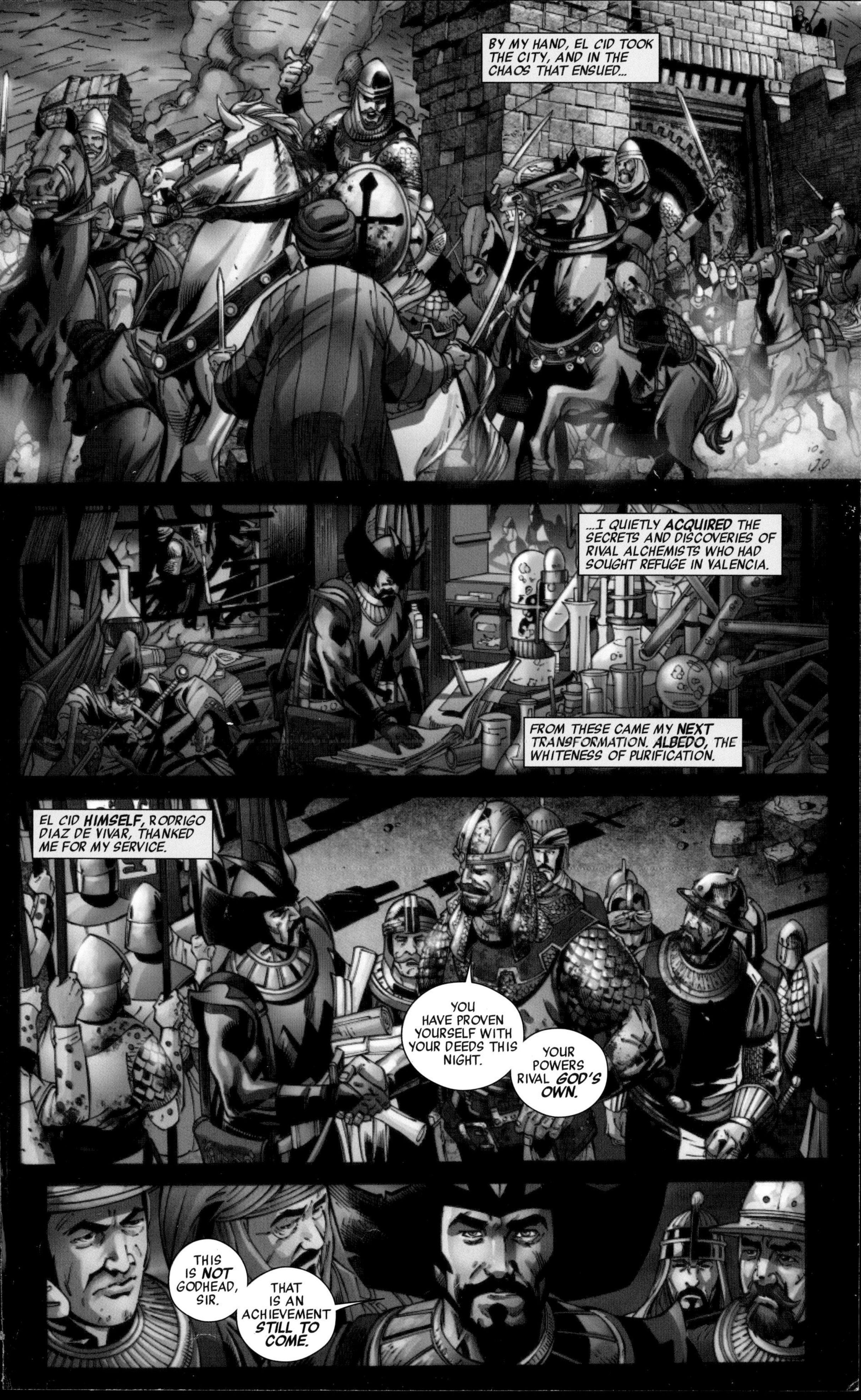
BY MY HAND, EL CID TOOK THE CITY, AND IN THE CHAOS THAT ENSUED...
...I QUIETLY ACQUIRED THE SECRETS AND DISCOVERIES OF RIVAL ALCHEMISTS WHO HAD SOUGHT REFUGE IN VALENCIA.
FROM THESE CAME MY NEXT TRANSFORMATION. ALBEDO, THE WHITENESS OF PURIFICATION.
EL CID HIMSELF, RODRIGO DIAZ DE VIVAR, THANKED ME FOR MY SERVICE.
YOU HAVE PROVEN YOURSELF WITH YOUR DEEDS THIS NIGHT.
YOUR POWERS RIVAL GOD'S OWN.
THIS IS NOT GODHEAD, SIR.
THAT IS AN ACHIEVEMENT STILL TO COME.

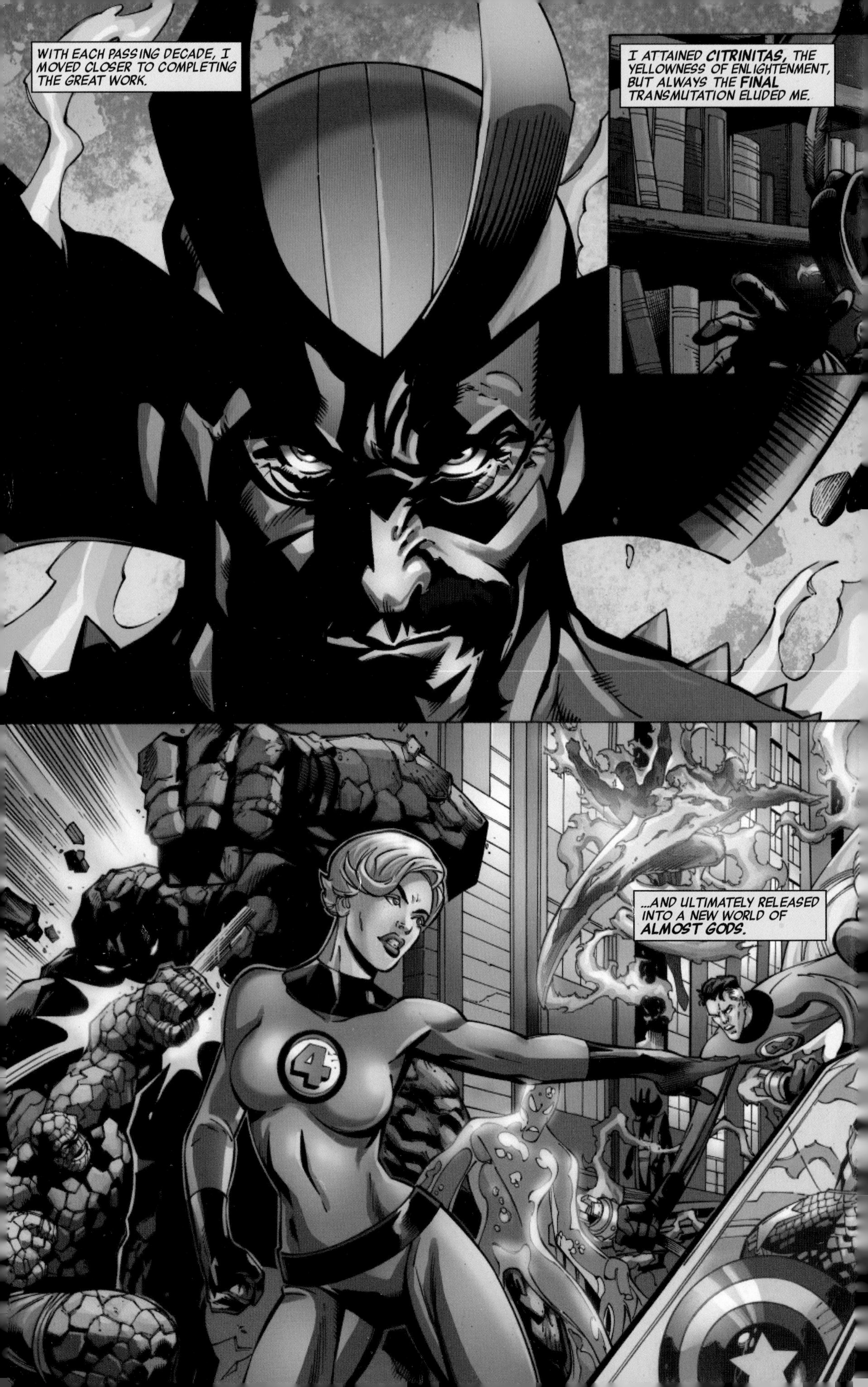
WITH EACH PASSING DECADE, I MOVED CLOSER TO COMPLETING THE GREAT WORK.
I ATTAINED CITRINITAS, THE YELLOWNESS OF ENLIGHTENMENT, BUT ALWAYS THE FINAL TRANSMUTATION ELUDED ME.
...AND ULTIMATELY RELEASED INTO A NEW WORLD OF ALMOST GODS.

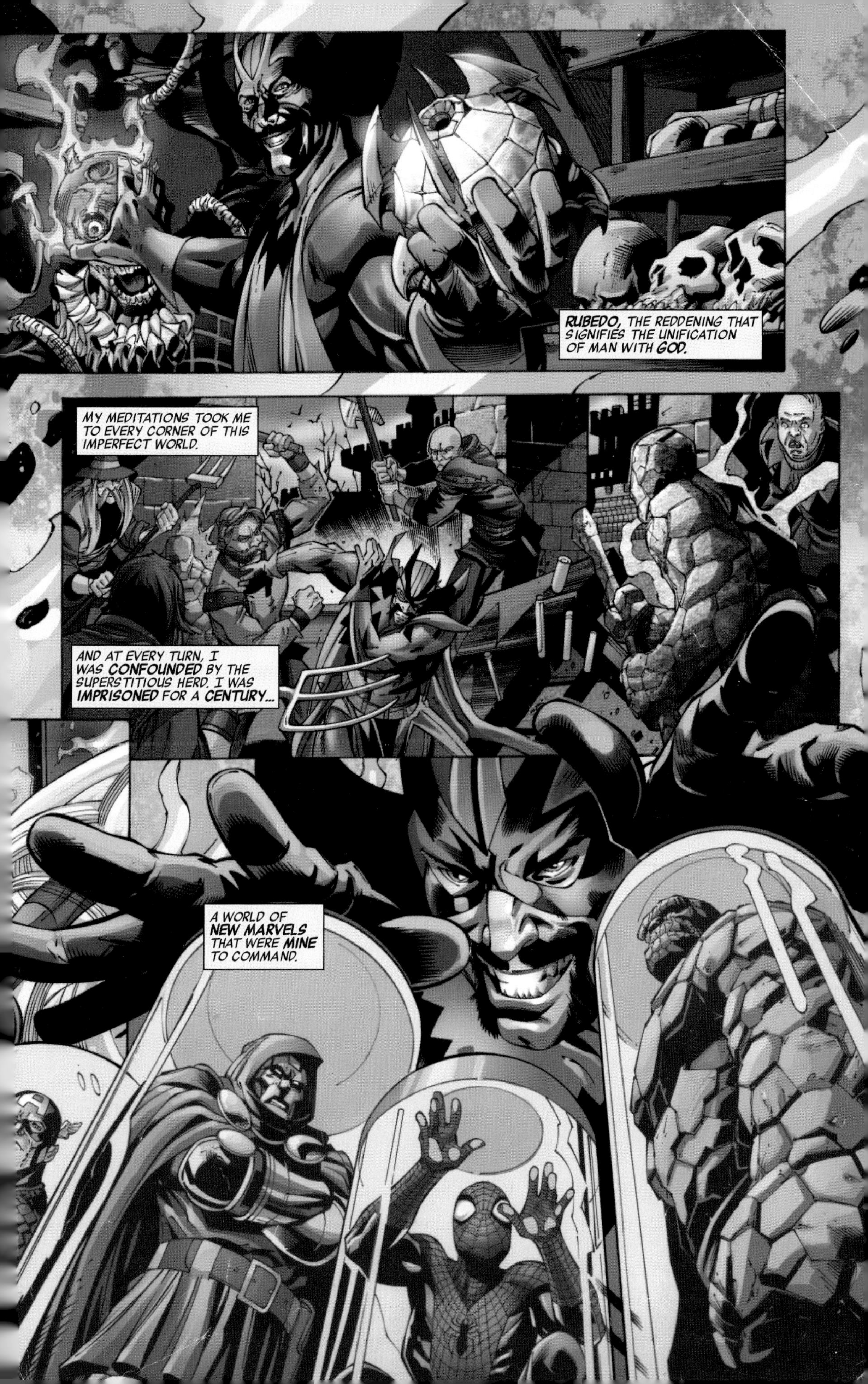
RUBEDO, THE REDDENING THAT SIGNIFIES THE UNIFICATION OF MAN WITH GOD.
MY MEDITATIONS TOOK ME TO EVERY CORNER OF THIS IMPERFECT WORLD.
AND AT EVERY TURN, I WAS CONFOUNDED BY THE SUPERSTITIOUS HERD. I WAS IMPRISONED FOR A CENTURY...
A WORLD OF NEW MARVELS THAT WERE MINE TO COMMAND.

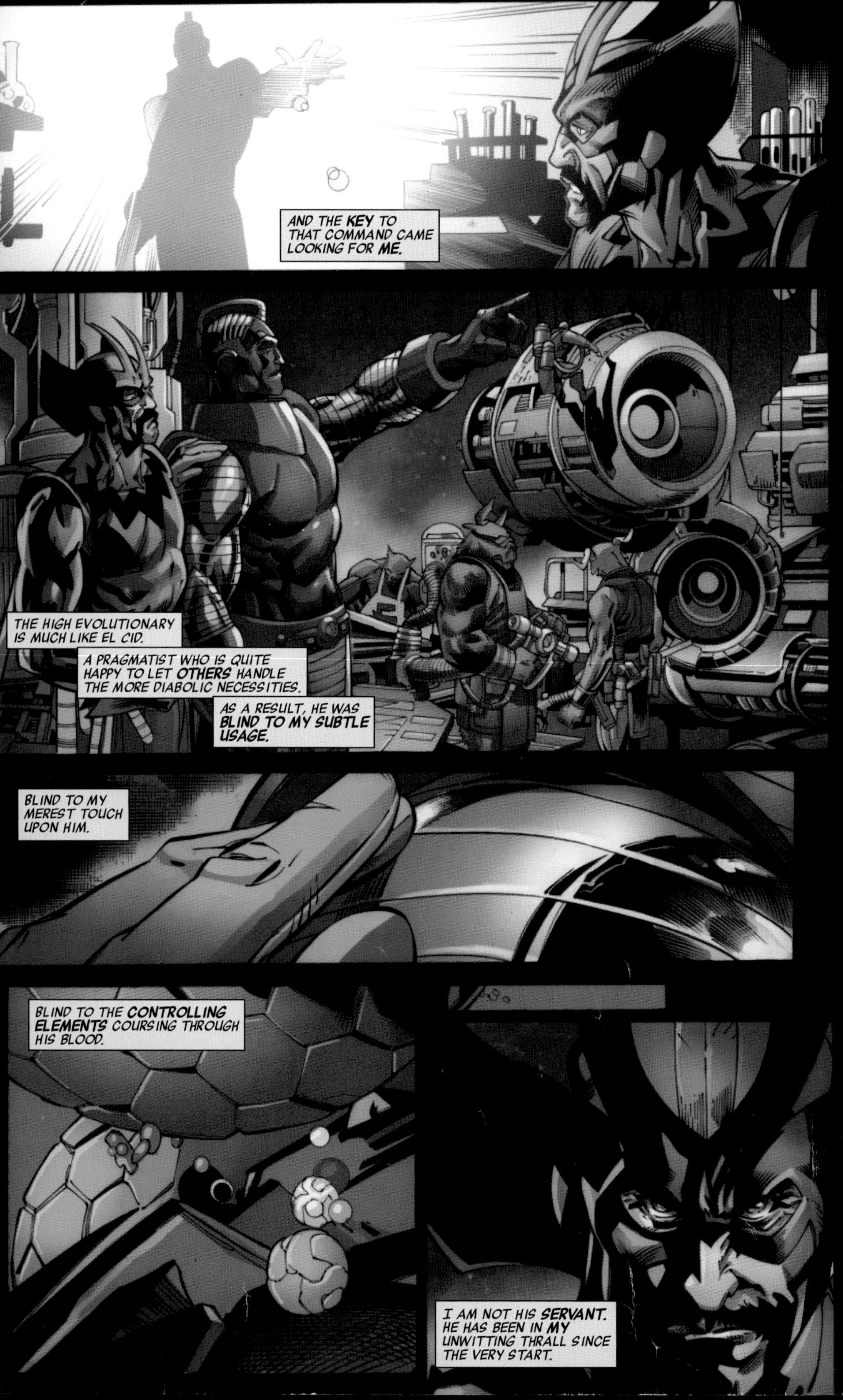
AND THE KEY TO THAT COMMAND CAME LOOKING FOR ME.
THE HIGH EVOLUTIONARY IS MUCH LIKE EL CID.
A PRAGMATIST WHO IS QUITE HAPPY TO LET OTHERS HANDLE THE MORE DIABOLIC NECESSITIES.
AS A RESULT, HE WAS BLIND TO MY SUBTLE USAGE.
BLIND TO MY MEREST TOUCH UPON HIM.
BLIND TO THE CONTROLLING ELEMENTS COURSING THROUGH HIS BLOOD.
I AM NOT HIS SERVANT. HE HAS BEEN IN MY UNWITTING THRALL SINCE THE VERY START.

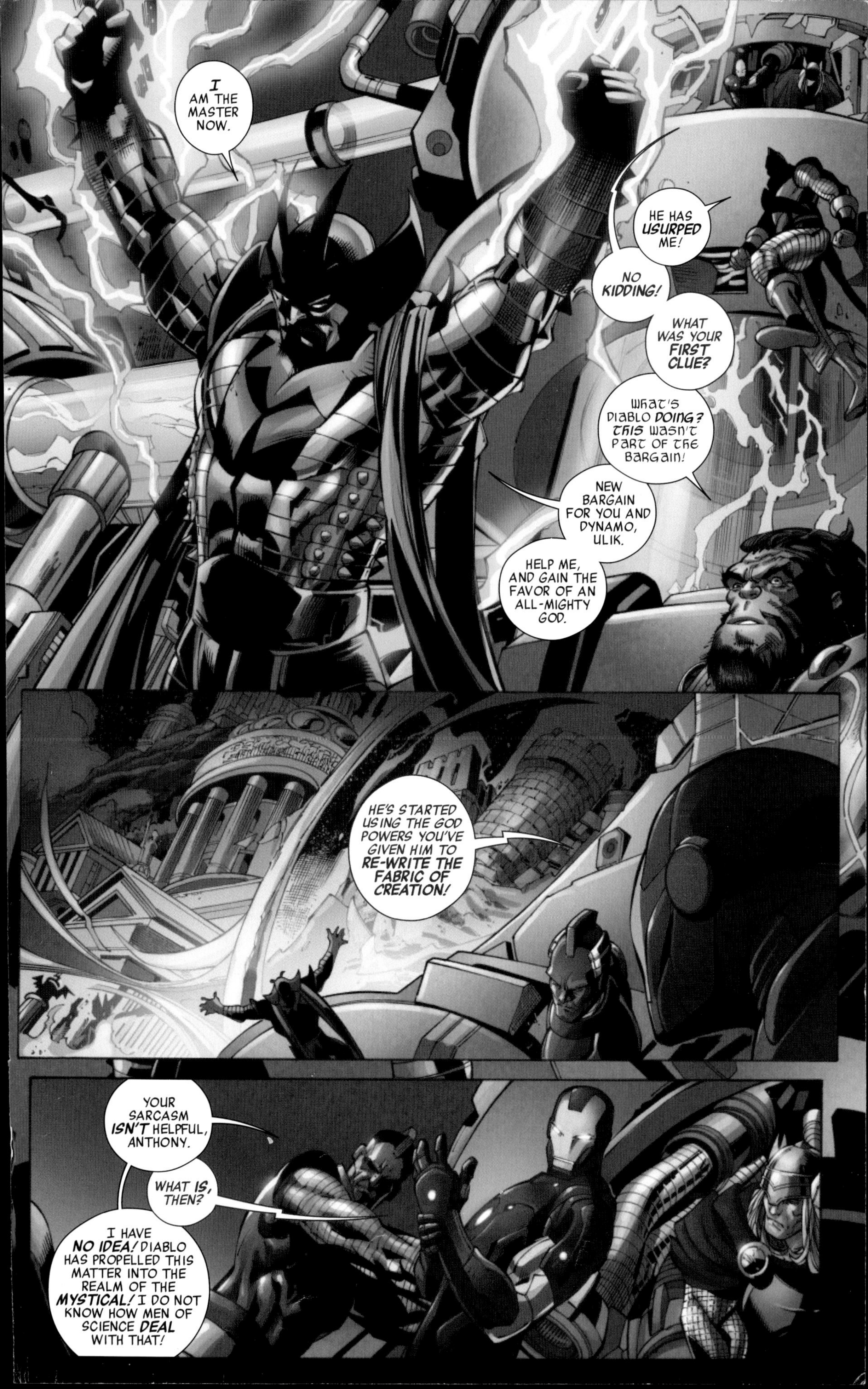
I AM THE MASTER NOW.
HE HAS USURPED ME!
NO KIDDING!
WHAT WAS YOUR FIRST CLUE?
WHAT'S DIABLO DOING? THIS WASN'T PART OF THE BARGAIN!
NEW BARGAIN FOR YOU AND DYNAMO, ULIK.
HELP ME, AND GAIN THE FAVOR OF AN ALL-MIGHTY GOD.
HE'S STARTED USING THE GOD POWERS YOU'VE GIVEN HIM TO RE-WRITE THE FABRIC OF CREATION!
YOUR SARCASM ISN'T HELPFUL, ANTHONY.
WHAT IS, THEN?
I HAVE NO IDEA! DIABLO HAS PROPELLED THIS MATTER INTO THE REALM OF THE MYSTICAL! I DO NOT KNOW HOW MEN OF SCIENCE DEAL WITH THAT!

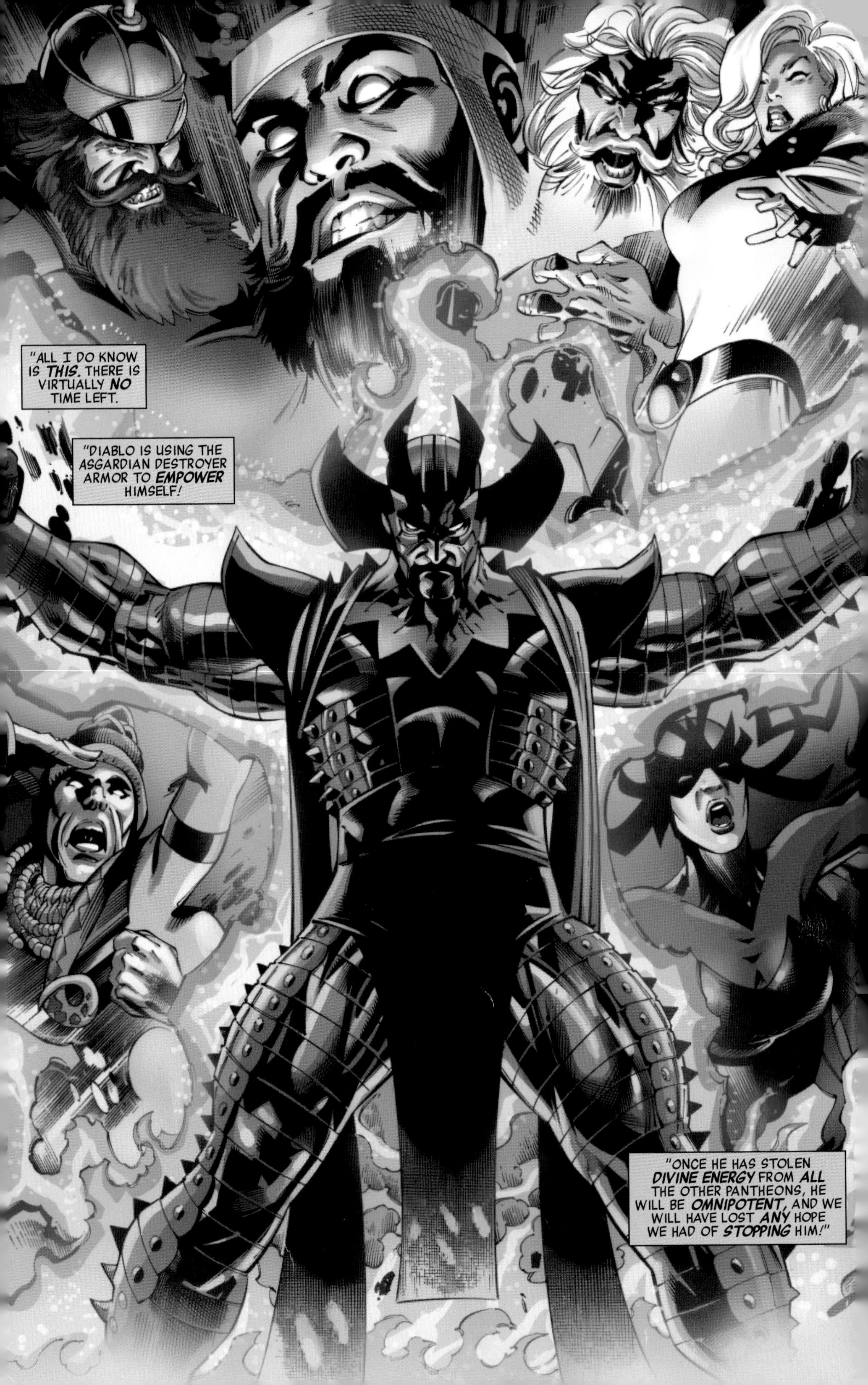
"ALL I DO KNOW IS THIS. THERE IS VIRTUALLY NO TIME LEFT.
"DIABLO IS USING THE ASGARDIAN DESTROYER ARMOR TO EMPOWER HIMSELF!
"ONCE HE HAS STOLEN DIVINE ENERGY FROM ALL THE OTHER PANTHEONS, HE WILL BE OMNIPOTENT, AND WE WILL HAVE LOST ANY HOPE WE HAD OF STOPPING HIM!"

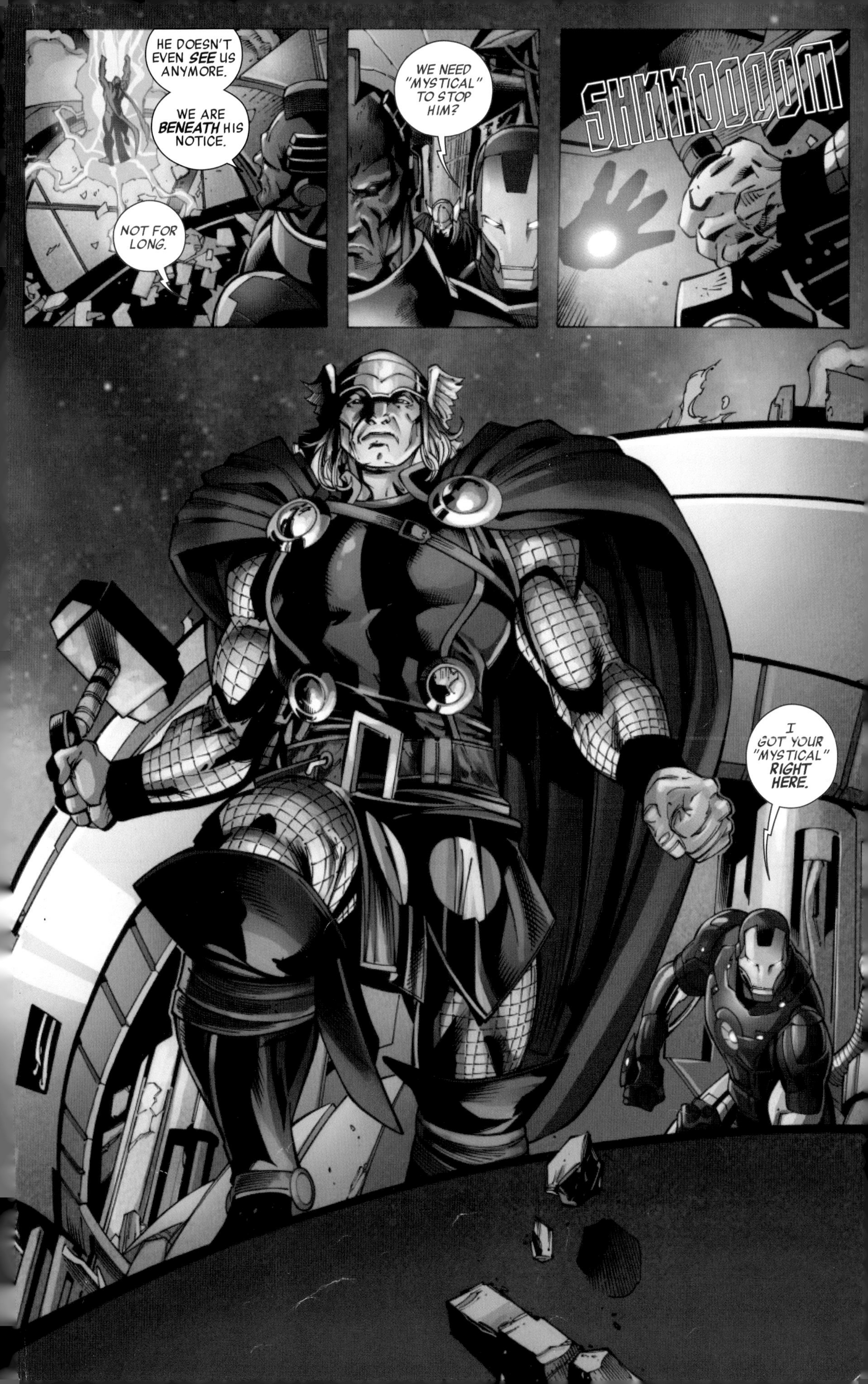
HE DOESN'T EVEN SEE US ANYMORE.
WE ARE BENEATH HIS NOTICE.
NOT FOR LONG.
WE NEED "MYSTICAL" TO STOP HIM?
SHKKOOOOM
I GOT YOUR "MYSTICAL" RIGHT HERE.

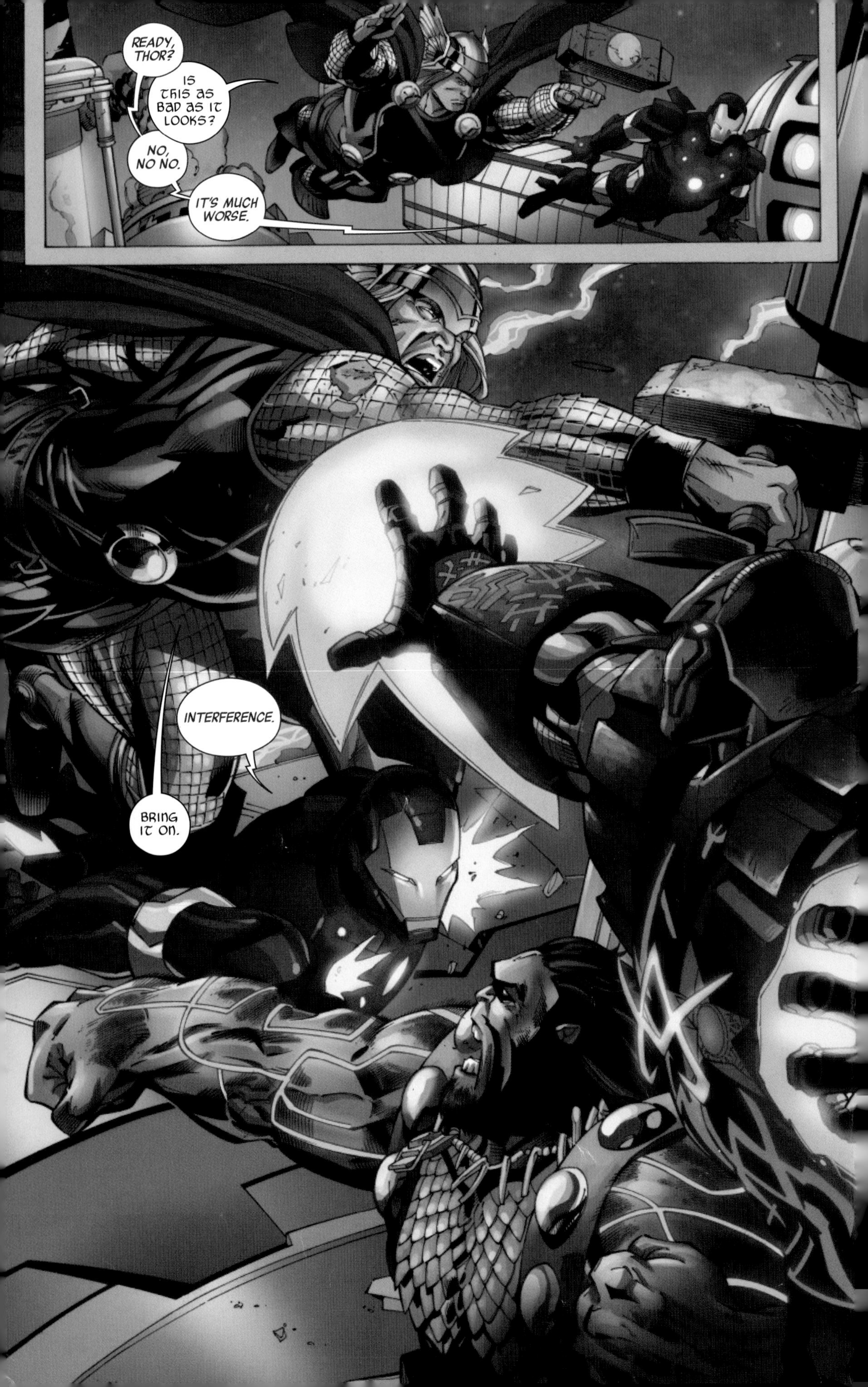
READY, THOR?
IS THIS AS BAD AS IT LOOKS?
NO, NO NO.
IT'S MUCH WORSE.
INTERFERENCE.
BRING IT ON.

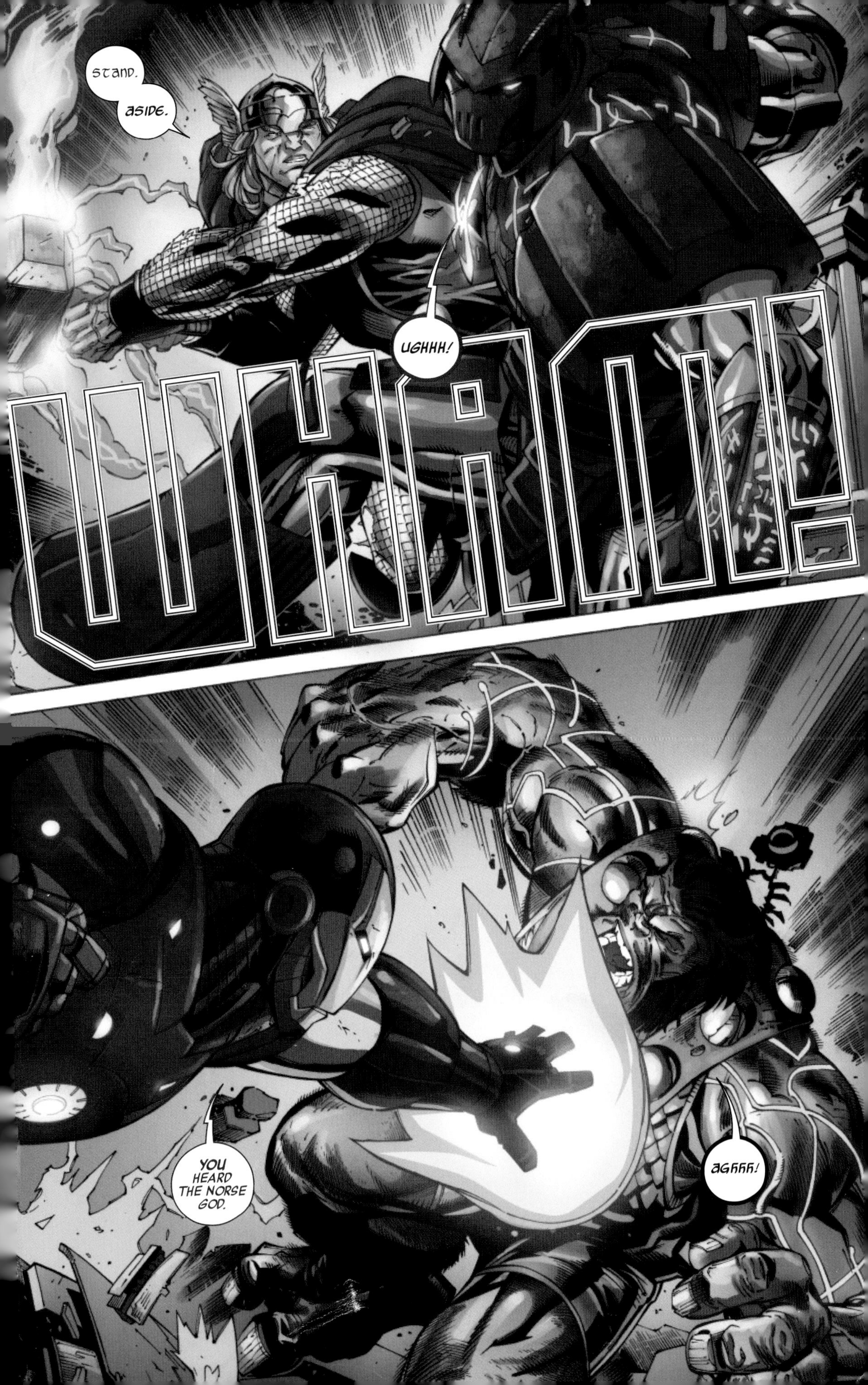
STAND.
ASIDE.
UGHHH!
WHAMM!
YOU HEARD THE NORSE GOD.
AGHHH!

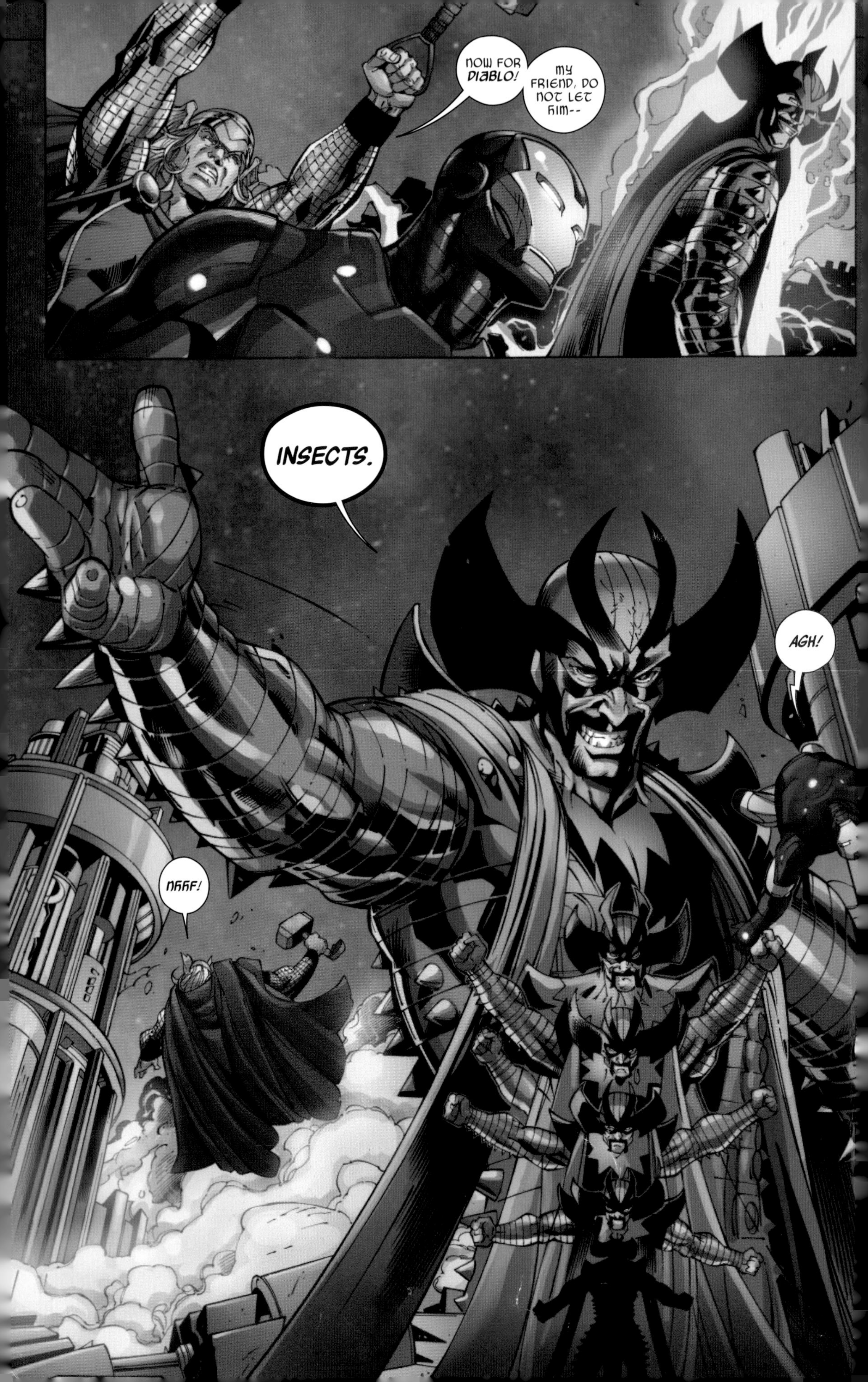
NOW FOR DIABLO!
MY FRIEND, DO NOT LET HIM--
INSECTS.
AGH!
NRRF!

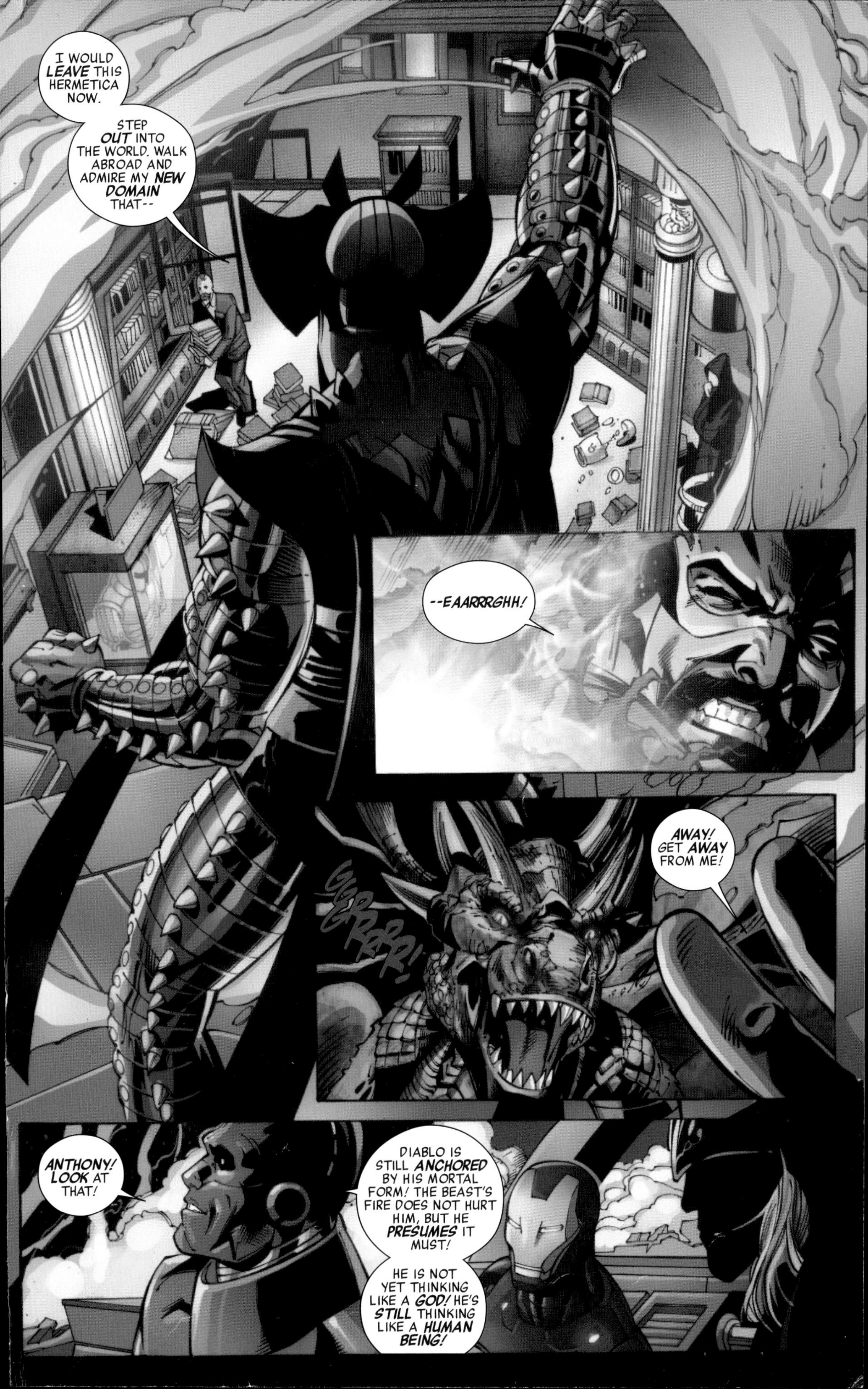
I WOULD LEAVE THIS HERMETICA NOW.
STEP OUT INTO THE WORLD. WALK ABROAD AND ADMIRE MY NEW DOMAIN THAT--
--EAARRRGHH!
GGRRRR!
AWAY! GET AWAY FROM ME!
ANTHONY! LOOK AT THAT!
DIABLO IS STILL ANCHORED BY HIS MORTAL FORM! THE BEAST'S FIRE DOES NOT HURT HIM, BUT HE PRESUMES IT MUST!
HE IS NOT YET THINKING LIKE A GOD! HE'S STILL THINKING LIKE A HUMAN BEING!

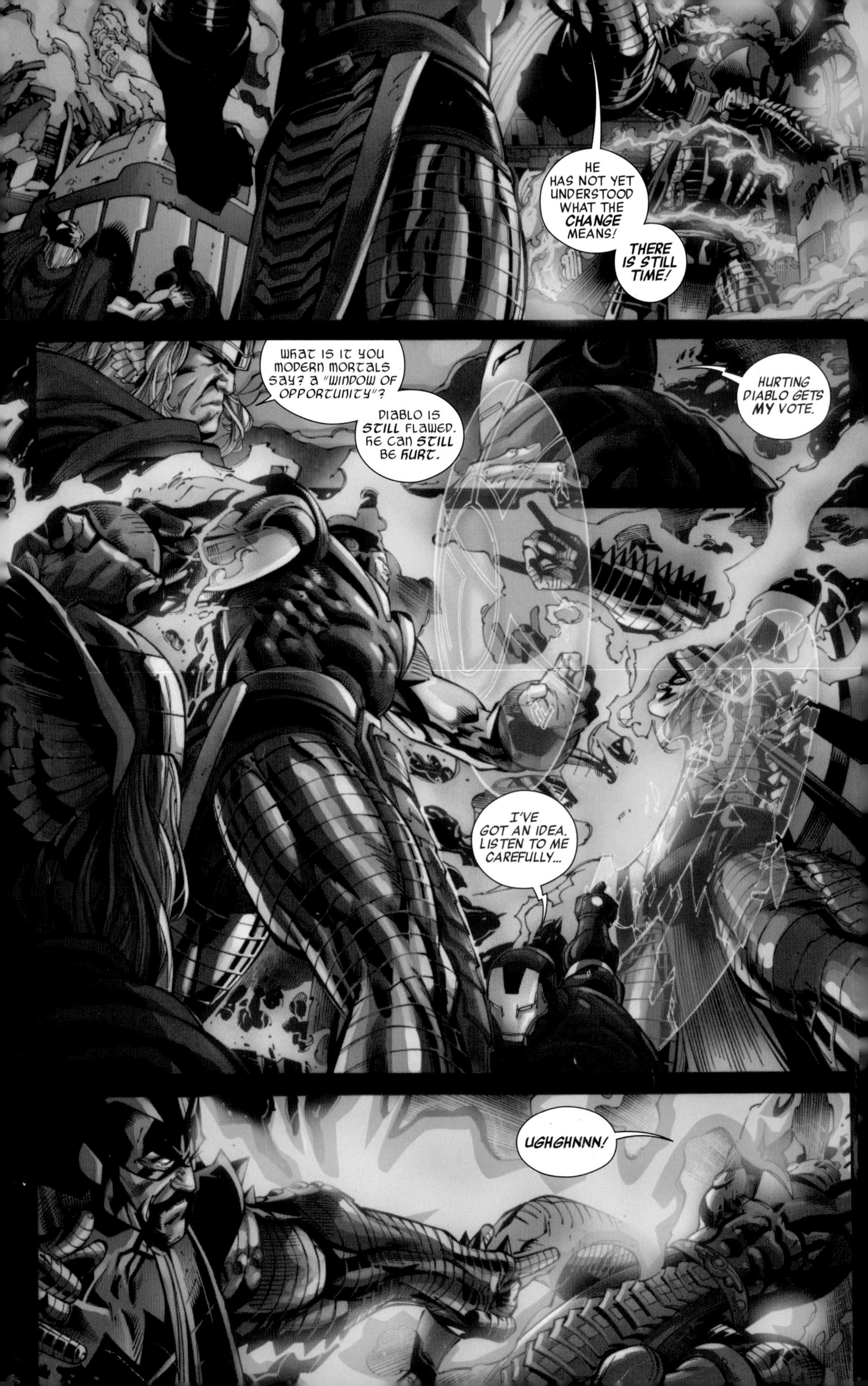
HE HAS NOT YET UNDERSTOOD WHAT THE CHANGE MEANS!
THERE IS STILL TIME!
WHAT IS IT YOU MODERN MORTALS SAY? A "WINDOW OF OPPORTUNITY"?
DIABLO IS STILL FLAWED. HE CAN STILL BE HURT.
HURTING DIABLO GETS MY VOTE.
I'VE GOT AN IDEA. LISTEN TO ME CAREFULLY...
UGHGHNNN!

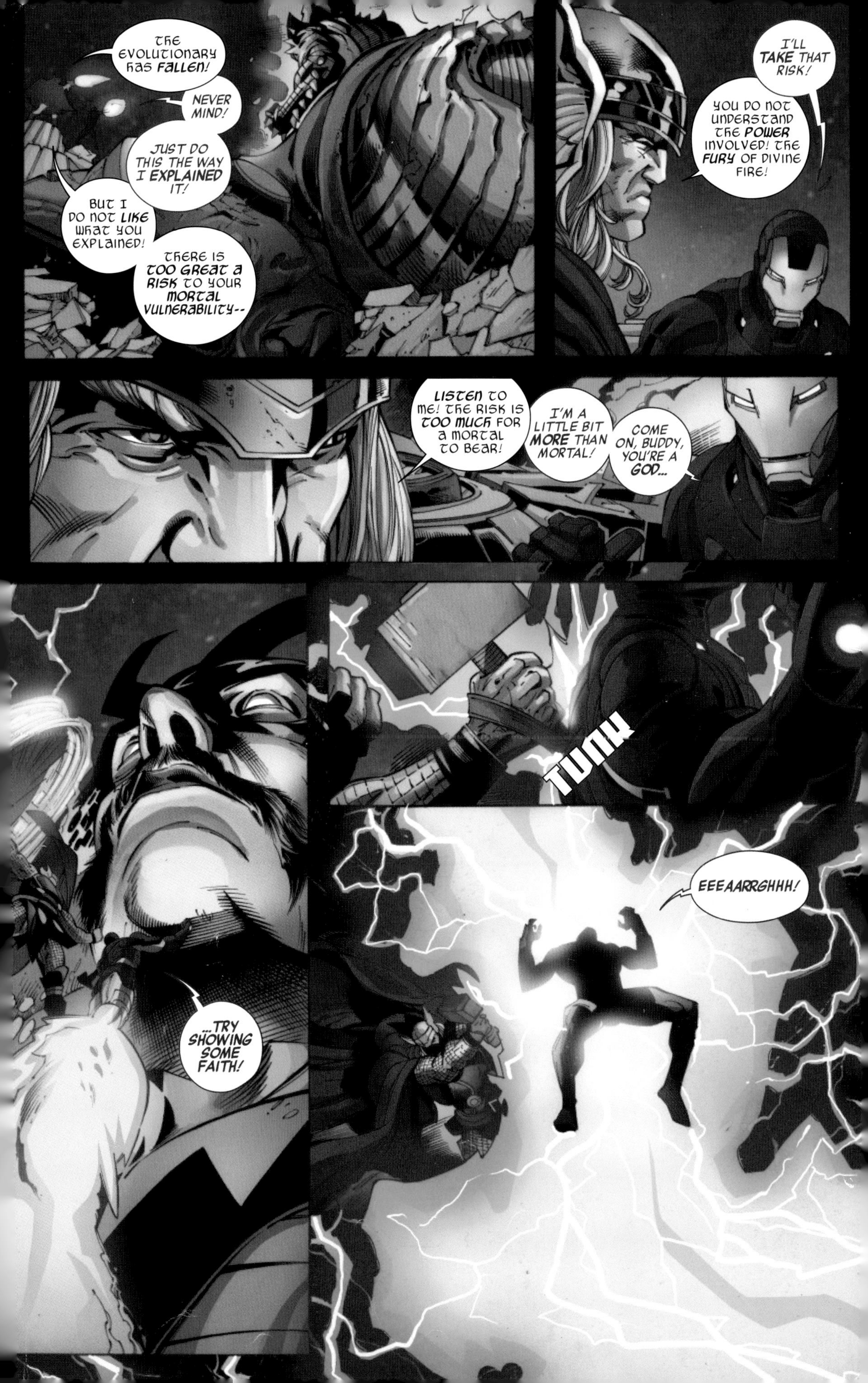
THE EVOLUTIONARY HAS FALLEN!
NEVER MIND!
JUST DO THIS THE WAY I EXPLAINED IT!
BUT I DO NOT LIKE WHAT YOU EXPLAINED!
THERE IS TOO GREAT A RISK TO YOUR MORTAL VULNERABILITY--
I'LL TAKE THAT RISK!
YOU DO NOT UNDERSTAND THE POWER INVOLVED! THE FURY OF DIVINE FIRE!
LISTEN TO ME! THE RISK IS TOO MUCH FOR A MORTAL TO BEAR!
I'M A LITTLE BIT MORE THAN MORTAL!
COME ON, BUDDY, YOU'RE A GOD...
...TRY SHOWING SOME FAITH!
TUNK
EEEAARRGHHH!

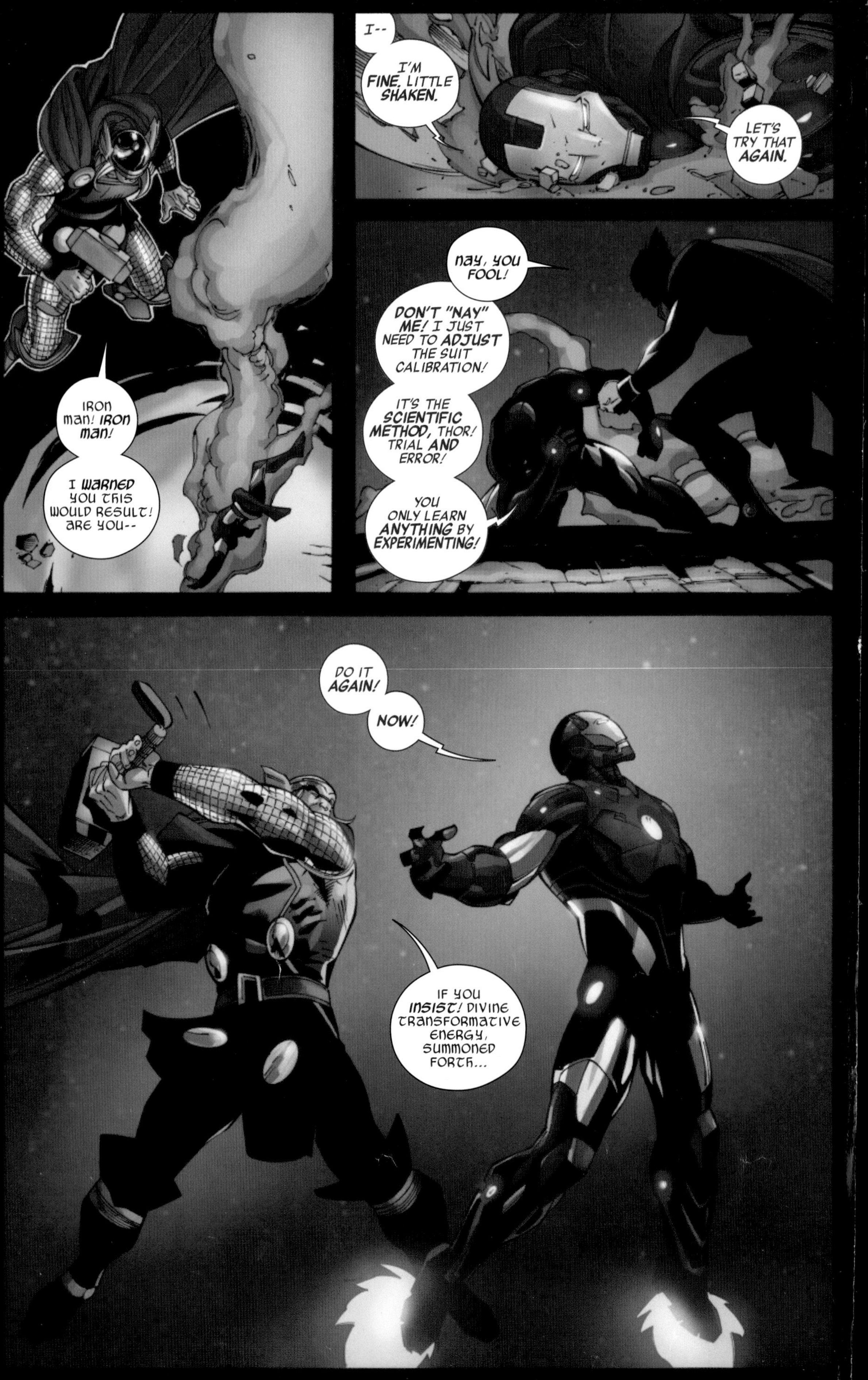
IRON MAN! IRON MAN!
I WARNED YOU THIS WOULD RESULT! ARE YOU--
I--
I'M FINE. LITTLE SHAKEN.
LET'S TRY THAT AGAIN.
NAY, YOU FOOL!
DON'T "NAY" ME! I JUST NEED TO ADJUST THE SUIT CALIBRATION!
IT'S THE SCIENTIFIC METHOD, THOR! TRIAL AND ERROR!
YOU ONLY LEARN ANYTHING BY EXPERIMENTING!
DO IT AGAIN!
NOW!
IF YOU INSIST! DIVINE TRANSFORMATIVE ENERGY, SUMMONED FORTH...

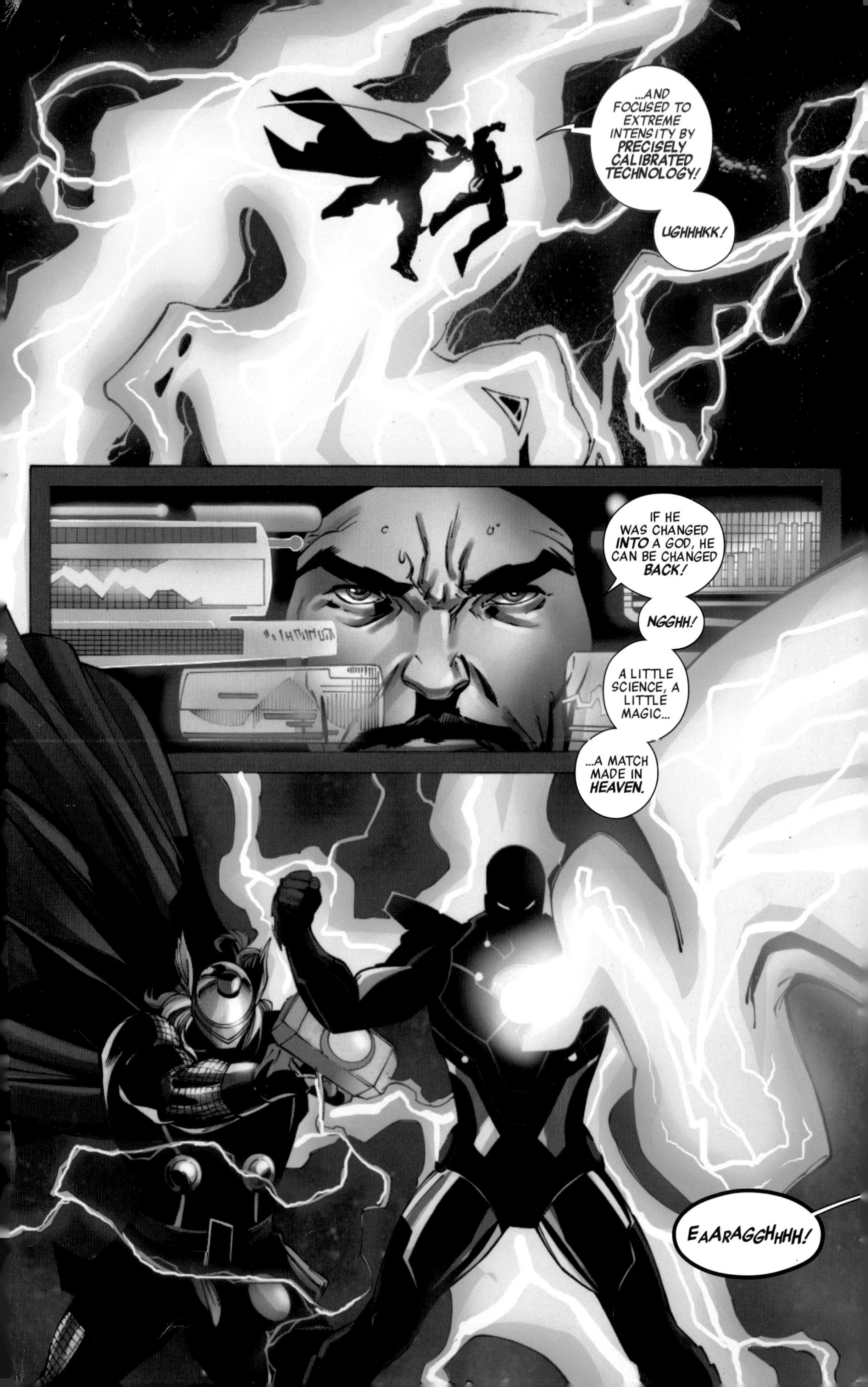

...AND FOCUSED TO EXTREME INTENSITY BY PRECISELY CALIBRATED TECHNOLOGY!
UGHHHKK!
IF HE WAS CHANGED INTO A GOD, HE CAN BE CHANGED BACK!
NGGHH!
A LITTLE SCIENCE, A LITTLE MAGIC...
...A MATCH MADE IN HEAVEN.
EAARAGGHHHH!

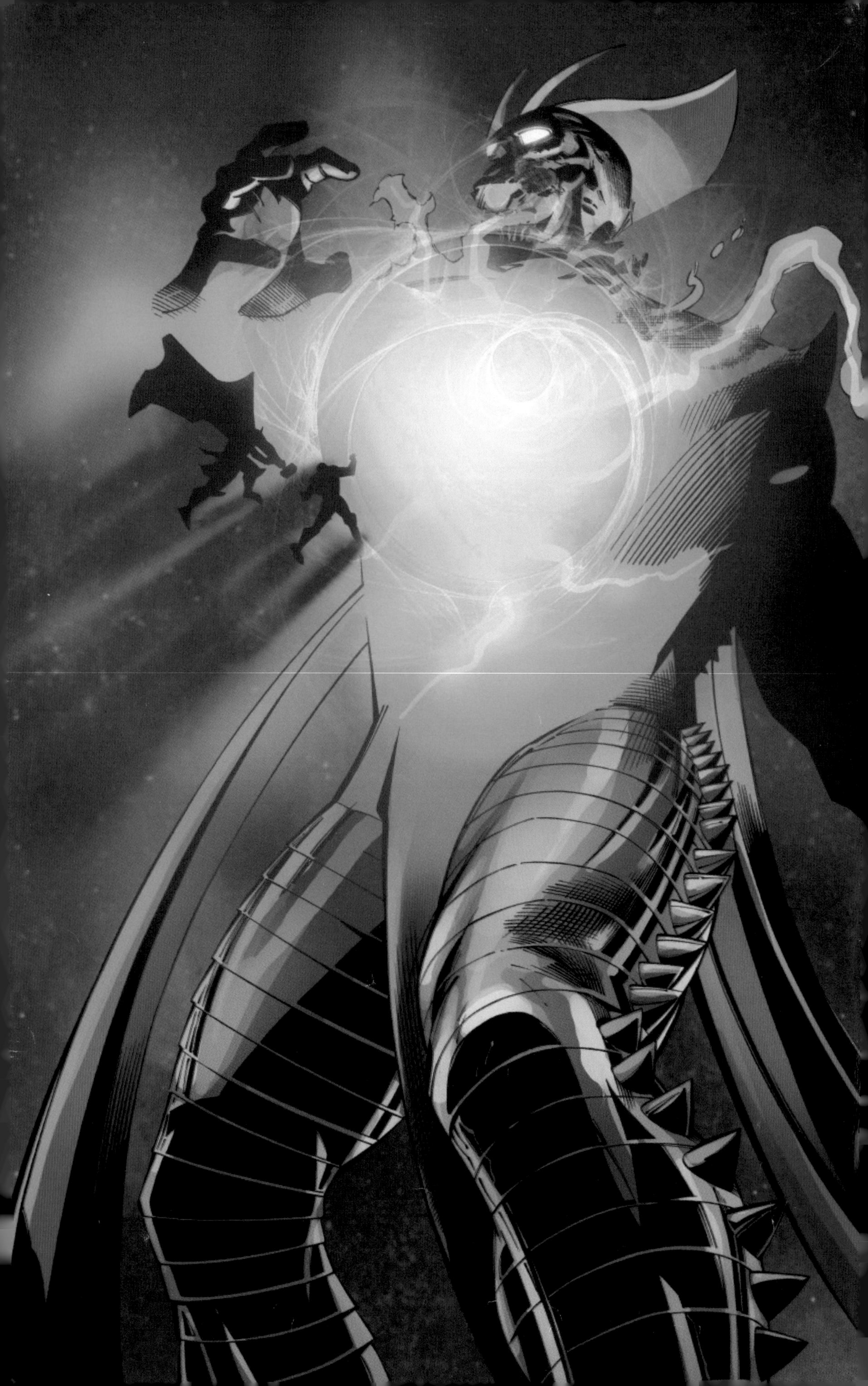

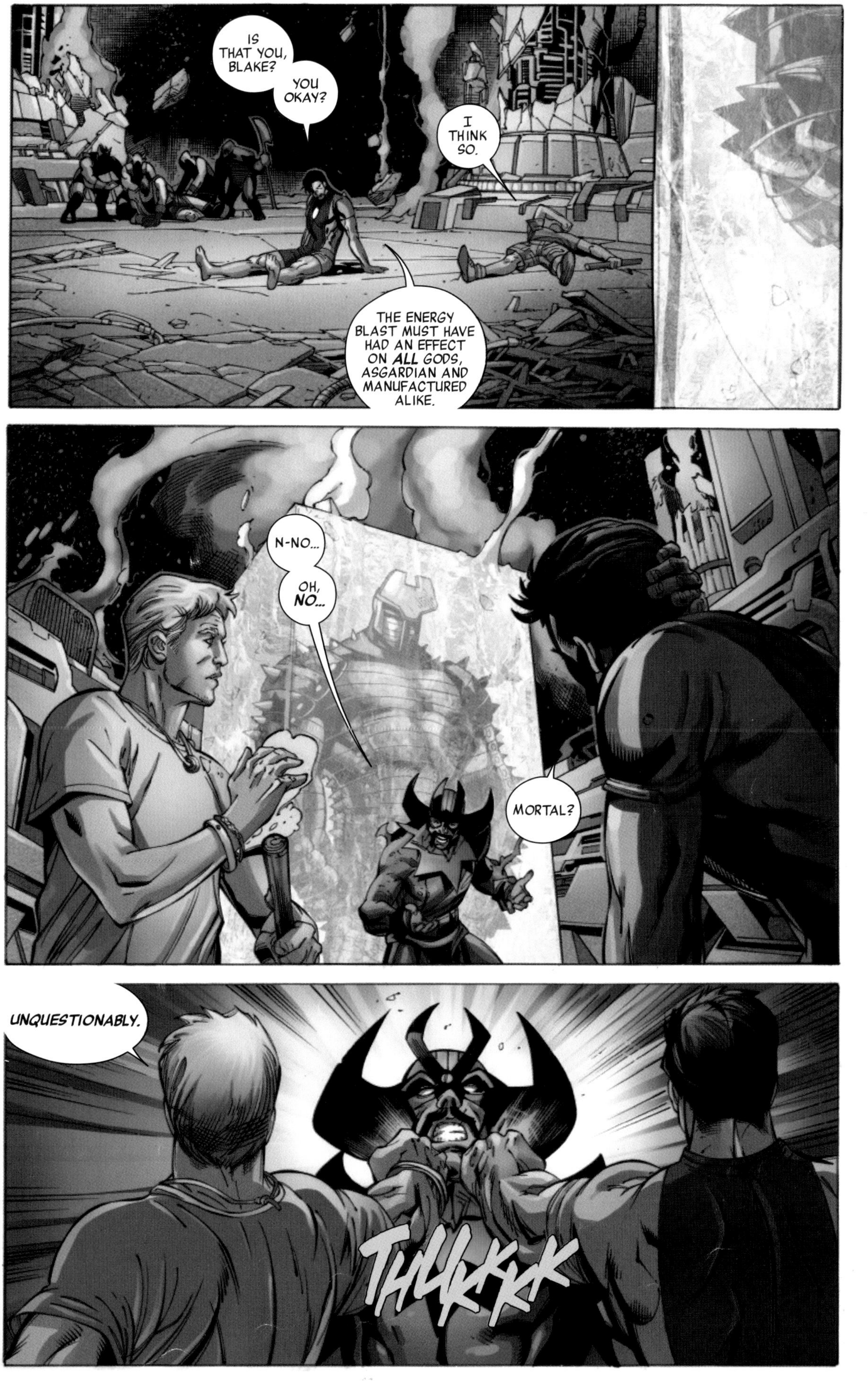
IS THAT YOU, BLAKE?
YOU OKAY?
I THINK SO.
THE ENERGY BLAST MUST HAVE HAD AN EFFECT ON ALL GODS, ASGARDIAN AND MANUFACTURED ALIKE.
N-NO...
OH, NO...
MORTAL?
UNQUESTIONABLY.
THUKKK

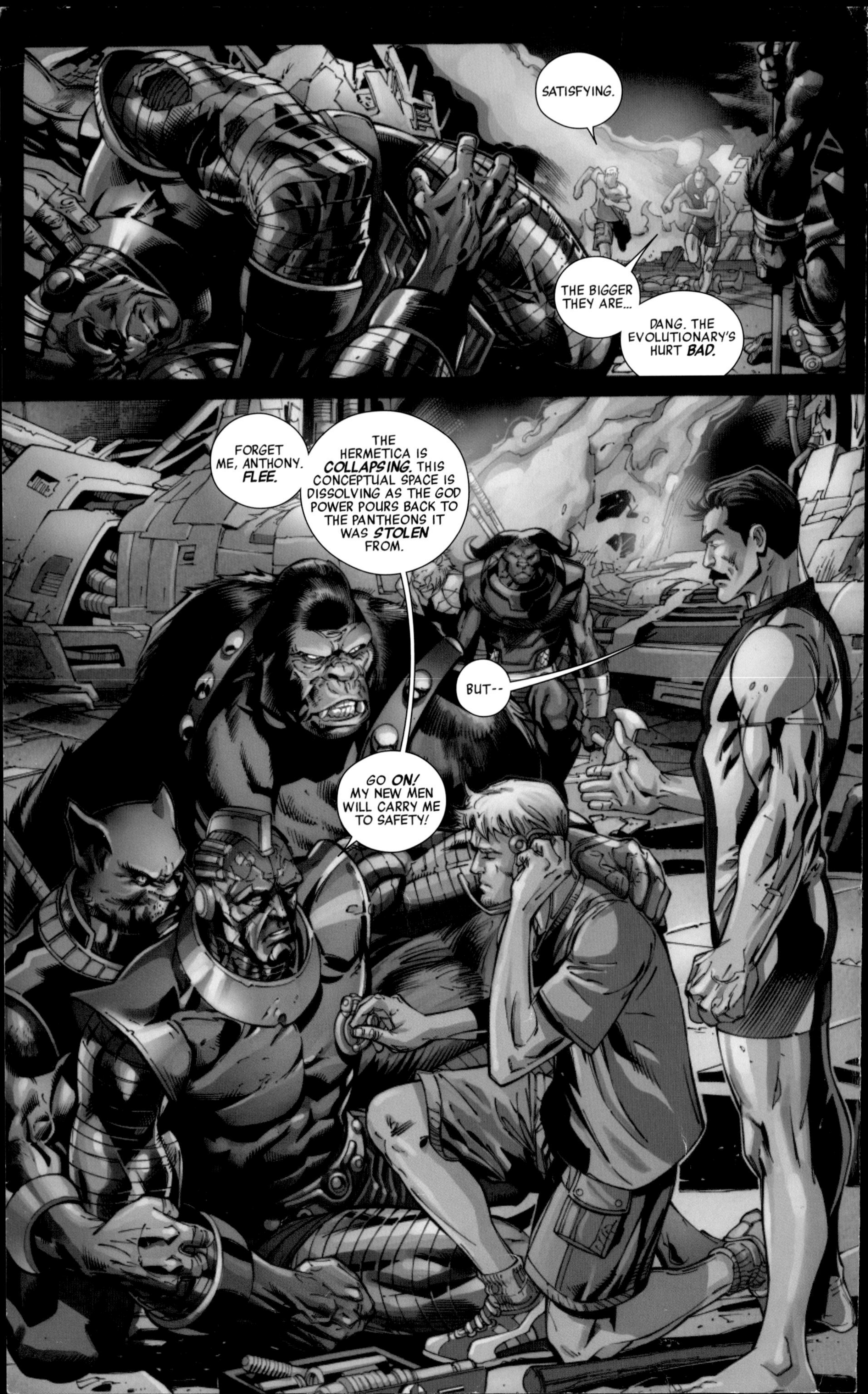
SATISFYING.
THE BIGGER THEY ARE...
DANG. THE EVOLUTIONARY'S HURT **BAD.**
FORGET ME, ANTHONY. **FLEE.**
THE HERMETICA IS **COLLAPSING.** THIS CONCEPTUAL SPACE IS DISSOLVING AS THE GOD POWER POURS BACK TO THE PANTHEONS IT WAS **STOLEN** FROM.
BUT--
GO **ON!** MY NEW MEN WILL CARRY ME TO SAFETY!

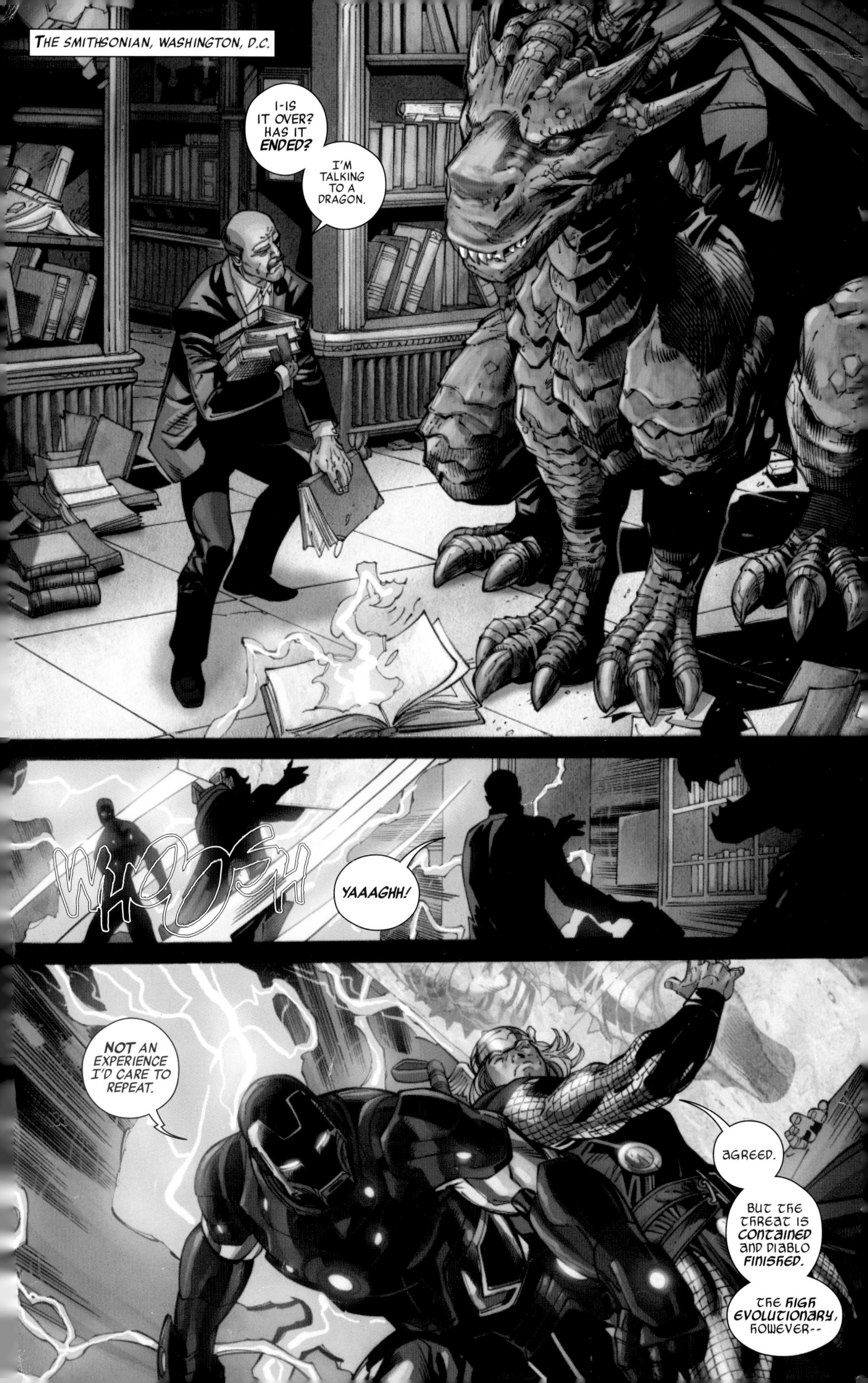

THE SMITHSONIAN, WASHINGTON, D.C.
I-IS IT OVER? HAS IT ENDED?
I'M TALKING TO A DRAGON.
WHOOSH
YAAAGHH!
NOT AN EXPERIENCE I'D CARE TO REPEAT.
AGREED.
BUT THE THREAT IS CONTAINED AND DIABLO FINISHED.
THE HIGH EVOLUTIONARY, HOWEVER--

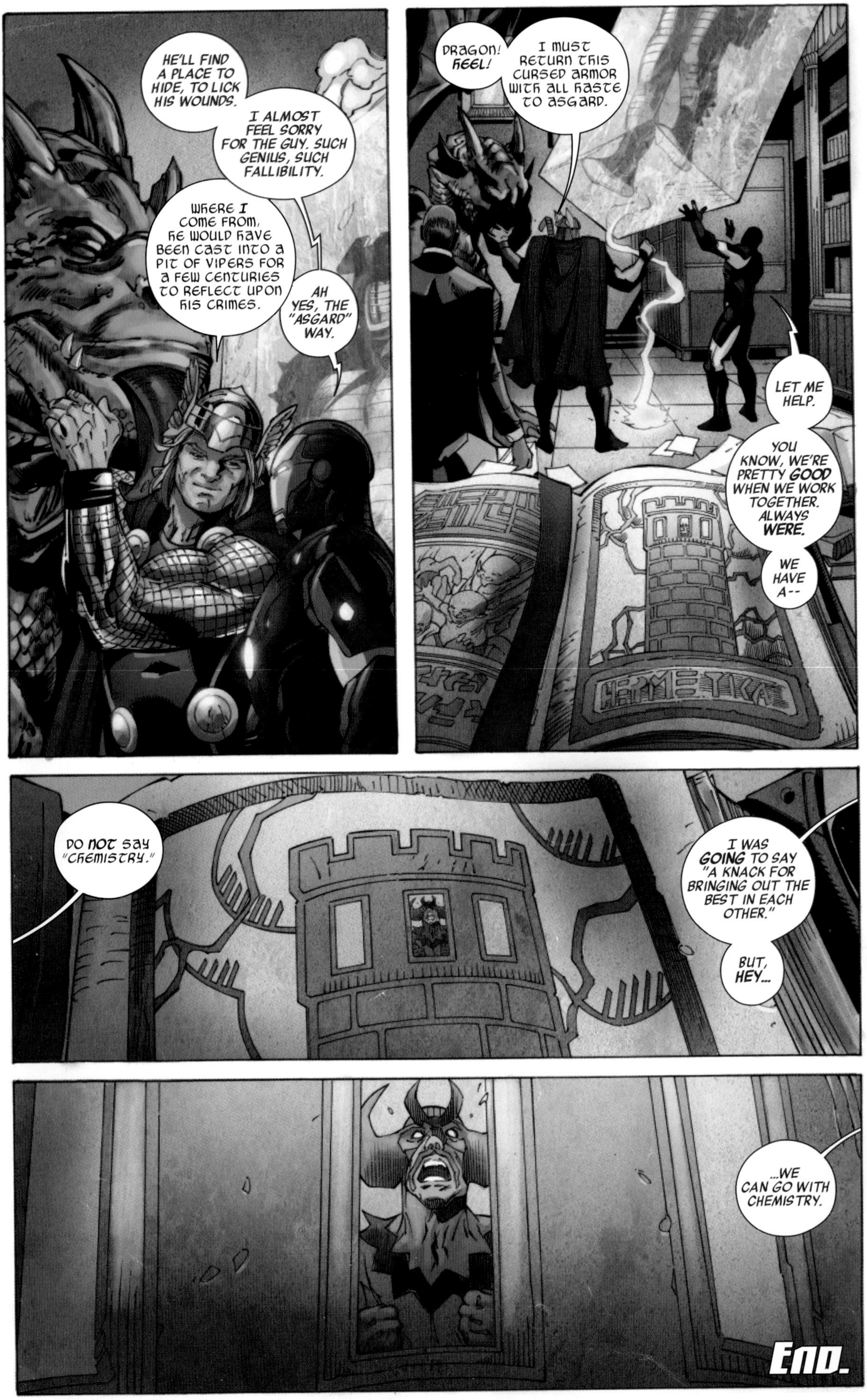
HE'LL FIND A PLACE TO HIDE, TO LICK HIS WOUNDS.
I ALMOST FEEL SORRY FOR THE GUY. SUCH GENIUS, SUCH FALLIBILITY.
WHERE I COME FROM, HE WOULD HAVE BEEN CAST INTO A PIT OF VIPERS FOR A FEW CENTURIES TO REFLECT UPON HIS CRIMES.
AH YES, THE "ASGARD" WAY.
DRAGON! HEEL!
I MUST RETURN THIS CURSED ARMOR WITH ALL HASTE TO ASGARD.
LET ME HELP.
YOU KNOW, WE'RE PRETTY GOOD WHEN WE WORK TOGETHER. ALWAYS WERE.
WE HAVE A--
HERMETIKA
DO NOT SAY "CHEMISTRY."
I WAS GOING TO SAY "A KNACK FOR BRINGING OUT THE BEST IN EACH OTHER."
BUT, HEY...
...WE CAN GO WITH CHEMISTRY.
END.